P9-BZO-570

Hugs and Kisses for The Grouchy Ladybug
Copyright © 2018 by Eric Carle LLC

www.harpercollinschildrens.com

ISBN 978-0-06-283568-0

Book design by Rachel Zegar
18   19   20   21   22   SCP   10   9   8   7   6   5   4   3   2   1
❖
First Edition

Hugs & Kisses

for The Grouchy Ladybug

By Eric Carle

HARPER

An Imprint of HarperCollinsPublishers

Hugs
and
kisses

will make you . . .

smile,

clap,

jump
for
joy,

stand tall,

and
swing
from
treetops.

You just might . . .

strut
your
stuff,

kick up

your

heels,

blush,

and
feel warm
and
fuzzy.

So remember, just like you . . .

even a
grouchy ladybug...

needs
hugs
and
kisses
too!

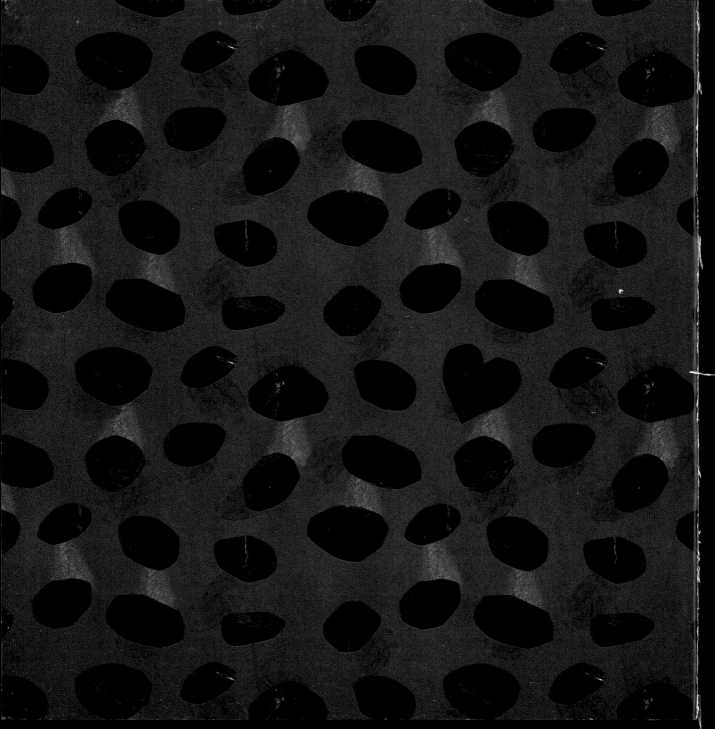